Ghost Horse Legend

Written and Illustrated by
Nancy J. Bailey

Dedicated to the Native Americans who love
this story, and to their horses.

There's a story the old ones tell by the fire,
When the stars are washed clean
in the wind,
When the coyotes sing out
beyond the cree jump,
When the echo of hoofbeats begin.

Mane and tails flying,
They run in the hills,
Just to follow the ghost stallion's flight.
Sorrel and grey, appaloosa and bay;
Are they real, or a dream in the night?

Now Traveler, he was very rich chief,
With an angry unscrupulous air.
He was friend to no man,
but his great pride and joy
Were fine horses that he wouldn't share.

Now Traveler, he had discovered one day
A new stallion had come to the pen.
It was dirty and white,
and had stood there all night.
It was old and so terribly thin.

He had no patience,
He had no heart,
So he beat the poor horse right to death.
He came back later on,
but the stallion was gone
And no sign of the body was left.

Now Traveler, he had a vision that night,
Glowing strong with a long mane and tail.
He said, "Traveler, you
have been tested like few;
And I'm afraid you have miserably failed."

Now Traveler jumped up and ran to the gate,
But his horses were gone, every one!
The vision that night said, "Follow the light
Until daybreak and there they will run."

"They will run, they will run!
For all day and all night they will run!"
The warning was clear, but he did not hear,
And now his long chase had begun.

Now Traveler follows the trail of his herd,
Over years and rough miles on the land.
The white stallion coaxes,
and taunts him with hoaxes,
But he never quite catches the band.
No, he never quite catches the band!

There's a story the old ones tell by the fire,
When the stars are washed clean
in the wind.
When the coyotes sing out
beyond the cree jump,
When the echo of hoofbeats begin.

Mane and tails flying,
They run in the hills
Just to follow the ghost stallion's flight.
Sorrel and grey, appaloosa and bay;
Are they real, or a dream in the night?

Are they real, or a dream in the night?

About the Author

Author, Artist, Bad Karaoke Singer, Nancy is the mom of a horse named Clifford who plays fetch and paints with watercolors. Clifford is the only horse in the world who signs his own biography, "Clifford of Drummond Island." He visits schools and libraries to promote literacy and respect for all living things.

CPSIA information can be obtained
at www.ICGtesting.com
Printed in the USA
LVHW072131260821
696238LV00014B/98